The Passover Parrot

Written by Evelyn Zusman
Illustrated by Katherine Janus Kahn

KAR-BEN COPIES, INC.   ROCKVILLE, MD

Library of Congress Cataloging in Publication Data

Zusman, Evelyn.
   The Passover Parrot.
   Summary: Relates what happens when the family parrot steals the afikomen at the Passover seder.
   [1. Passover — Fiction. 2. Jews — Rites and ceremonies — Fiction. 3. Parrots — Fiction]
I. Kahn, Katherine, ill. II. Title.
PZ7.Z84Pas 1984   [E]   83-22182
ISBN 1-58013-024-0 (pbk.)

Published by KAR-BEN COPIES, INC., Rockville, MD 1-800-4-KARBEN
Printed in the United States of America

I loved our brownstone house in Brooklyn. It had a large, homey kitchen and lots of room upstairs. Best of all was the big backyard with the tall oak tree that shaded us from the summer sun. My brothers Joey and Saul and I loved to play there, especially in the springtime.

One day our neighbor, Mrs. Brown, knocked on our door.

"Good morning," Mama said. "What's that you're holding? Your parrot!"

"Yes, Mrs. Cohen. I'm moving. Wouldn't you like to keep him?" She noticed me, tugging at Mama's skirt, and pushed the cage into my hand. "For you, Leba, a present."

And before Mama could say, "Seven children and a parrot!" Mrs. Brown was gone.

I jumped with such delight that I scared the parrot half to death. Mama shook her head. "More things to take care of," she grumbled.

"I'll help you, Mama. You'll see."

It was shortly before Passover, and Mama was cleaning the house, removing all the hametz, the leavened food we cannot eat on the holiday. She began to refer to the parrot as "that hamatzdikeh bird," and before long, we all called him "Hametz."

"Can you say the Four Questions in Hebrew?" Papa asked me a few days before the Seder.

His eyes and his smile seemed to say, "It's okay if you can't." But Joey was old enough to ask them in English, so I made up my mind to learn them in Hebrew.

"Mama, will you listen to me say the Four Questions?" I asked.

But Mama was too busy. "Go play in the yard, Leba. Joey will listen to you."

I asked Joey.

"Why me?" he said. "Ask Saul or Rachel or Fran."

"Never mind," I replied.

In the end I chose Hametz. He was never too busy to listen. In fact he loved it when I practiced. And practice I did — over and over again.

"*Mah nishtanah halailah hazeh...*" I sang. And Hametz repeated in his parrot-squeaky voice: "*Mah nishtanah halailah hazeh...*"

"*Mi kol halaylot,*" I continued.

"*Mi kol halaylot,*" squeaked the parrot.

Would Papa be surprised! I could hardly wait for the Seder.

At last the day came. David and Fran helped Mama in the kitchen. Rachel and Saul set the table. Joey, Becky, and I checked that every-thing was in order.

"Haggadot?" Joey asked.

"Check," I said.

"Charoset?"

"Mmm!" Becky said, sampling some.

"Wine?"

"Enough for every cup and Elijah's, too," Papa said, as he carried in the case.

The guests arrived. Everyone was so dressed up. After we admired the table, we took our places, and Papa began the Seder.

He broke the middle matzah and put half back under the satin cover. He wrapped the other half in a napkin. "This is the Afikomen," he said, as he slipped it behind his pillow. "It means dessert. Whoever finds it will get a reward."

We all smiled.

"Don't worry," Saul whispered to me. "I'll take it when Papa is busy singing. Then I'll give it to you, Leba."

Joey laughed. He had already taken the Afikomen. "Here, Leba. Hide it quickly," he whispered.

I snatched the napkin with the Afikomen and ran upstairs to my bedroom. As I slipped back into my seat, Papa called, "Quiet, everyone. Leba will ask the Four Questions."

I stood on a chair and began to sing: *"Mah nishtanah halailah hazeh..."*

And as I paused to take a breath, Hametz, who had been sitting quietly in his cage in the living room, repeated in his squeaky parrot voice: *"Mah nishtanah halailah hazeh..."*

All eyes turned to Hametz. I tried to continue.

"Mi kol halaylot."

The parrot squeaked right after me, *"Mi kol halaylot."* My brothers giggled. The guests laughed, too.

"Take the parrot up to the bedroom," Papa ordered.

I did as he said.

When I came back I sang the Four Questions without a single mistake. The guests clapped, and Papa smiled.

The sweet singing and the delicious meal took all my attention, and I soon forgot the parrot.

At last, Papa called for the Afikomen so we could finish the Seder.

"Joey, do you have it?"

"No, Papa."

"Saul, do you have it?"

"No, Papa."

"Leba?"

"Yes, Papa."

"May I have it please."

I ran to my bedroom, but there was no Afikomen. I looked under the table and under the bed. No Afikomen. And there was no parrot, either. The cage door was wide open and Hametz was gone.

I sat down on the floor and began to cry. Papa sent Joey, and he searched, too. Then came Saul. In a minute, he knew exactly what had happened.

"Follow me," he said.

Joey and I followed him down the stairs, through the kitchen, and out the back door into the yard.

There was Hametz,
perched on a branch of
our tall oak tree, holding
the Afikomen tightly in
his beak.

"Somebody has to climb the tree," Saul said.

"You'd better go," said Joey. "I might tear my new pants."

"No, don't go," I said. "Let me just talk to Hametz."

Then, at the top of my lungs, I sang as loudly as I could, *"Mah nishtanah halailah hazeh..."*

Hametz couldn't resist. He opened his beak and repeated word for word, *"Mah nishtanah..."* The Afikomen dropped.

DID JOEY CATCH IT?

DID SAUL?

You'll never believe it, but I CAUGHT IT MYSELF! Well, what was left of it. When I turned around, the whole family and all our guests were standing and watching and clapping.

Mah nishtanah halailah hazeh mi kol halaylot...

As we returned to the house to finish the Seder, we heard echoes of a squeaky voice singing, *"Mah nishtanah..."* Hametz had flown quietly back through the window into the cage. Perched on one leg, he was practicing for the second night's Seder.